# Make Way for Princess Cora

by Joshua Smith

Dedicated to my wife for her love and support and to my son who has a fantastic imagination.

"Follow my lead, kid." Cora said. "We don't have much time before your mom picks you up, but I know just what we should play."

Ali leaned in close to Cora. Actually, a little too close. Cora needed personal space for her imagination to grow.

Cora stood tall with her hands on her hips. "I am Princess Cora, The Kindhearted!"

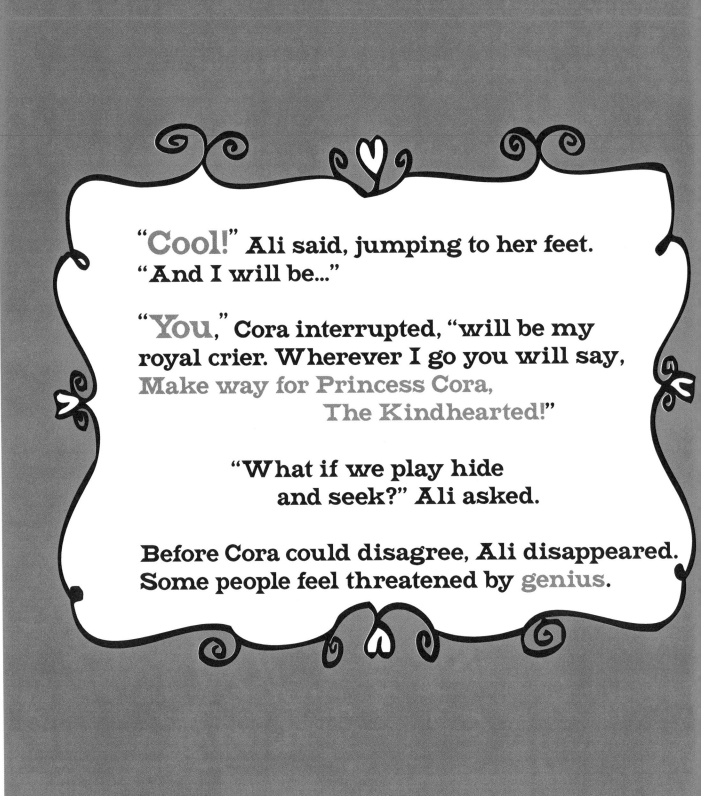

"Cool!" Ali said, jumping to her feet. "And I will be..."

"You," Cora interrupted, "will be my royal crier. Wherever I go you will say, Make way for Princess Cora,
                    The Kindhearted!"

"What if we play hide
        and seek?" Ali asked.

Before Cora could disagree, Ali disappeared. Some people feel threatened by genius.

A shadowy figure stood out among the laundry that rippled on the clothes lines.
Pink boots gave away Ali's hiding spot.

"Gotcha!" Cora yelled, throwing the hanging bed sheet above her head.

There were Ali's pink boots, but the figure was a decoy.

**"No, I got You!"**
Ali said, looking down
on Cora from the
tree house window.

**"Now it's your turn, Cora.
I'll give you to the count of
ten to hide."**

Cora stood her ground with her arms crossed the whole time Ali counted.

"Ready or not, here I..." Ali said, uncovering her eyes.

Cora frowned at Ali's dumbfounded expression. "This is **NOT** how you play princess." She said, stomping her foot.

"Come down from there right now!"

Ali disappeared from the window into the tree house.

"Girls!" Mommy announced, "lunch is ready."

Cora went into the house and returned with two peanut-butter and jelly sandwiches.

"Yummy!" Cora said through a full mouth. "PBJ is food fit for royalty. Of course I would share with my royal crier."

Any minute now Ali would scurry down the tree house ladder and beg to share PBJs with her royal highness, Princess Cora.

Instead, laughter erupted from the tree house. What's that kid up to? Cora thought, climbing the tree house ladder.

"Oh Mr. Dashy," Ali said to a bear in a top hat, "you've outdone yourself with this tea party."

"What's all this?" Cora demanded.

But Ali didn't answer. It was like she was in her own little world and Cora didn't even exist.

"Don't worry about burning the biscuits, Mrs. Tweedle." Ali continued, talking to a rag doll. "The oven's light bulb is notoriously too hot."

"I just wanted this to be a perfect tea party." Mrs. Tweedle said. Then the rag doll began sobbing.

# "Boo-hoo, boo-hoo-hoo!"

"You couldn't have arrived at a better time."
Ali suddenly said to Cora. "Be a dear and fetch
Mrs. tweedle a handkerchief before her tears
flood the house."

Cora placed the PBJ on the table and offered
the handkerchief to the rag doll in hopes of
ending this madness.

"Boo-hoo, boo-hoo-hoo!"
Mrs. Tweedle just kept sobbing.

"She's already soaked the handkerchief clean through!" Ali said. "The house is flooding. Quickly, use the teacups to bail the water out the window!"

Cora helped Ali furiously bail water until they were huffing and puffing.

"It's... no... use!" Ali said, catching her breath. "We have to get her to stop crying."

"I know," Cora said. "We can just bake more biscuits."

"By the time they bake," Ali replied, "we'll have floated half way around the world."

"Too bad all I brought along was this." Cora said, dangling the PBJ sandwich from her hand like a dirty rag.

"Good thinking." Ali said, high-fiving Cora.

Cora held the plate while Ali cut the sandwich into bite sized portions.

"What do you have there?" Mrs. Tweedle sniffled through her sobbing.

Cora held the plate of bite sized PBJs in front of the rag doll.

"Mrs. Tweedle," Ali said, "her royal highness, Princess Cora, The Kindhearted has brought us a delicacy from her home land."

Cora curtsied and said, "Go ahead, try one."

"Delicious!" Mrs. Tweedle declared. "Her royal highness has saved the tea party!"

Cora blushed. "It was nothing."

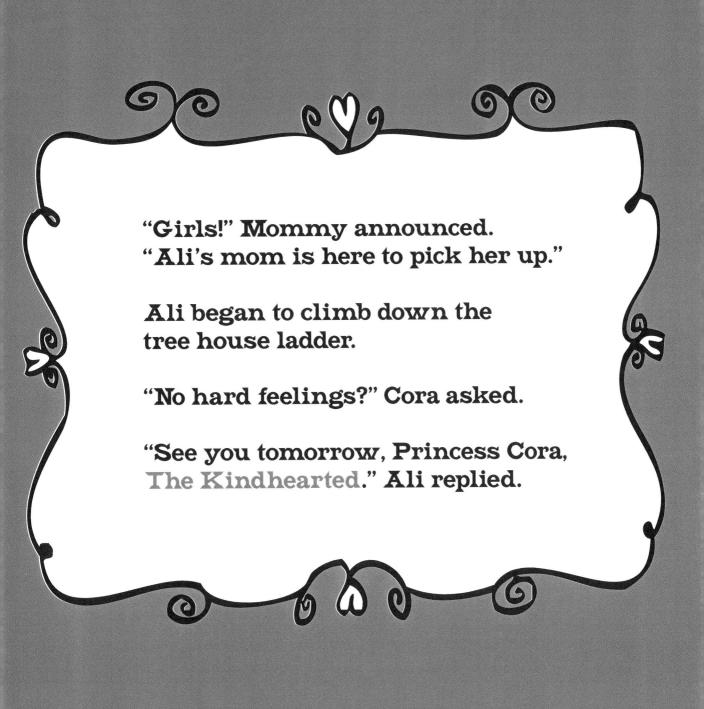

"Girls!" Mommy announced.
"Ali's mom is here to pick her up."

Ali began to climb down the
tree house ladder.

"No hard feelings?" Cora asked.

"See you tomorrow, Princess Cora,
The Kindhearted." Ali replied.

As Ali ran to her mom's car, Cora leaned
out the tree house **window yelling,**

"Make way for Ali,
The Wonderful!"

This is my first published picture book. I've written stories and made art since I was a kid and I hope to make, and publish, many more.

My wife and I, along with our son call Springboro, Ohio our home. We have deep roots in the buckeye state, and a family tree with branches in the blue grass state as well.

If you are a curious reader--and no doubt you are--you noticed that this story takes a few inspirations from the book, *Alice's Adventures in Wonderland* by Lewis Carroll. I'd be excited to know which Alice references you find, so ask mom or dad to help you email me just for fun! My email is princesscorabook@gmail.com. Don't worry mom and dad, this isn't a trick to get your email address so I can send you a bunch of spam--that would be rude. If you want updates on my future work, find out how to sign up for my newsletter on the next page.

Happy reading,
Joshua Smith

Stay in touch!
Sign up for email updates on
Joshua's future books.
joshuasmithbooks.com

Made in the USA
Lexington, KY
06 January 2017